F

IS FOR

FINALLY

FOREWORD

The life of a Chicago Cubs fan has never been an easy one. After being a powerhouse that won 8 championships from 1876 to 1908, the Cubs continued to get close for years and years. They won back-to-back championships in 1907 and 1908 and appeared in 7 more through 1945. Then the Cubs just stopped winning. The Curse of the Billy Goat was thought to be the culprit. The truth is, it was a combination of bad owners, bad players, and bad managing. They lost and they lost and they lost. Meanwhile, the fans, easily the most loyal and dedicated in all of sports, waited and waited and waited. Generations of Cubs fans begged and prayed that this would be their year. And many fans never lived to see what we witnessed in 2016.

My grandfather was born in 1913 and died in 2010 and, through 97 long years, never saw the Cubs win it all. This book is not just for the fans who witnessed the miracle of 2016 or the young fans who we are bringing into the Cubs family. This book is for the memory of all the Cubs fans who never got to feel the magic we all felt in 2016. For me, it is for my grandfather, who we called Boppy; for my mother, who took me to countless games and had so much fun with baseball even though she never saw them even get to a World Series; and for my wife's Uncle Denny, a man whose happy-go-lucky attitude toward life and the Cubs now lives on with his kids. We all have family and friends who we loved and lost who loved the Cubs as they lost. Most of all, this book is dedicated to my beautiful children, Ivy and William Waveland. We hope they see many, many more championships in the years to come!

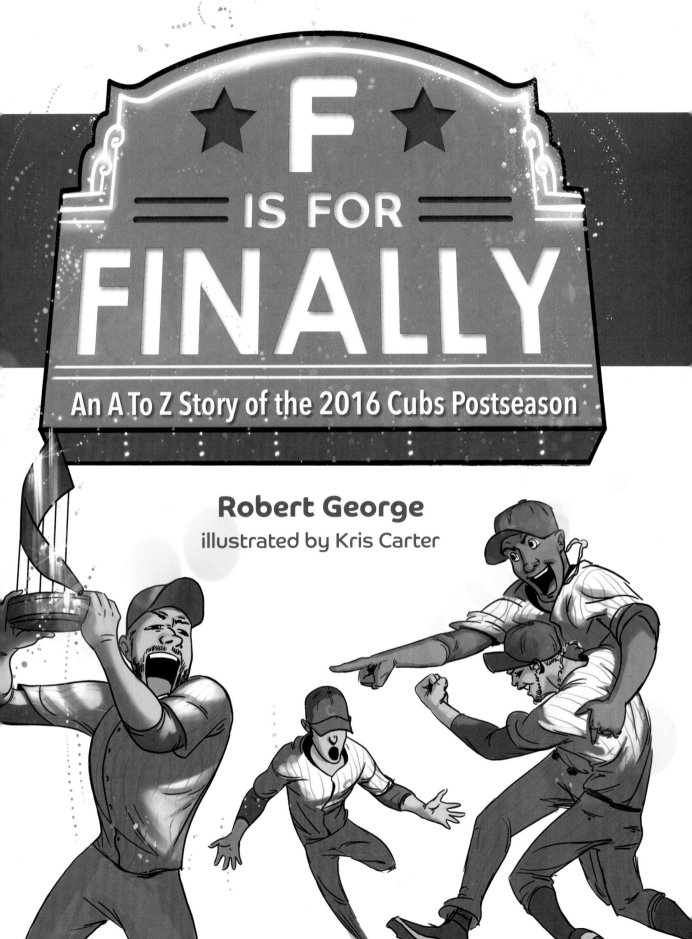

F IS FOR FINALLY

An A To Z Story of the 2016 Cubs Postseason

Robert George

illustrated by Kris Carter

Aa

is for Almora

A is for Almora, who we'll call on
to start the **fun.**
He came into the 10th of Game 7
and scored the winning **run.**

Albert Almora was Theo
Epstein and company's
first ever draft pick for
the Cubs.

Bb is for Baez

B is for Baez, manning the second base **bag.**
He ends every catcher's throw with an amazing **tag.**

Javier Baez became known for his acrobatic tags at second base during the 2016 season.

Cc

is for Chapman

Pitcher	Pitch Speed (mph)	
Chapman, Aroldis	103.0	
Chapma	103.9	
Chapman,	3.6	
Chapman, Aroldis	102.9	
Chapman, Aroldis	102.	
Chapman, Aroldis		
Chapman, A	101.4	
	103.9	

C is for Chapman, the man at the end of the **game.** His fastball hits 105. That's his claim to **fame.**

MLB's Statcast had to create a Chapman filter for the fastest pitches because he throws so much harder than anyone else.

Dd is for Delay

D is for Delay, when the Cubs were filled with **fear.**
By the time Jason Heyward spoke, they knew this was their **year.**

After giving up the lead in the 8th, the rain delayed the game heading into the 10th inning. Jason Heyward lifted the spirits of the entire team before they came back out to win the final game.

Ee

is for Emotion

E is for Emotion, it's in a glass **case.**
You can read it from Rizzo's lips or on every Cubs fan's **face.**

Anthony Rizzo used the classic line from the movie *Anchorman* to describe how he felt to David Ross during Game 7.

Ff is for Fowler

F is for Fowler, who streaks the bases with a **burst.** But in the final game, he homered in the **first.**

Dexter Fowler was more known for his speed, but his power ignited the Cubs to start the clinching game.

Gg is for Goat

G is for Goat, the source of Cubs fans' **ire,** whose own fate was set the day of Epstein's **hire.**

The famous Billy Goat Curse was placed in 1945 by a man who was not allowed to bring his pet goat into a World Series Game. The curse said the Cubs would never appear in another World Series again.

Hh is for Hendricks

H is for Hendricks and his crafty Dartmouth **brain.**
Hitters think they have a chance—a thought that is **insane.**

Known to teammates as the Professor, Kyle Hendricks out-thinks hitters to make up for his lack of velocity.

Ii

is for the Ivy

I is for the Ivy that grows on the Wrigley **wall.**
It has never looked more beautiful than at the end of **fall.**

In 1937, Bill Veeck planted ivy on the outfield walls, where it still grows today.

Jj is for Joe Maddon

J is for Joe Maddon, the brain behind the **brawn,** whose crafty, goofy leadership helped the curse be **gone.**

Joe Maddon is a manager who knows how to keep things light. He has pajama parties, live zoo animals at practice, and dance parties after every win.

K k is for Kyle Schwarber

K is for Kyle Schwarber, thought to be lost to the **team.**
His brave return at bat made real our wildest **dream.**

Kyle Schwarber badly injured his knee and was not expected to play until the following season.

Ll is for **Lackey and Lester**

L is for Lackey and Lester, old folks in this **clan,** who pitched like 20-somethings to complete Theo's **plan.**

John Lackey, 38 years old, and Jon Lester, 32, added veteran leadership to a very young team.

M is for MVP

NL MVP

WORLD SERIES MVP

M is for MVP,
   both KB and **Ben,**
the pair that fueled a magic season
   we may see soon **again.**

Kris Bryant became the first player in history to win College Player of the Year, Minor League Player of the Year, Rookie of the Year, and Most Valuable Player in consecutive seasons. Ben Zobrist took the World Series MVP for his steady play and decisive hit in the 10th inning of Game 7.

Nn

is for
Next year

WRIGLEY FIELD
HOME OF
CHICAGO CUBS

2016 WORLD CHAMPS!

N is for Next year, no longer from **1908.**
After 108 years, it was surely worth the **wait.**

The Cubs motto had always been "Wait 'Til Next Year," because they always came up short.

Oo is for Outfield

O is for Outfield, where the angels now are **merry.** With big cheers and "Holy Cows!" from Banks to Ron to **Harry.**

The Angels in the Outfield for the Cubs are Harry Caray, the iconic voice of the Cubs for many years, Mr. Cub Ernie Banks, and fellow Hall of Fame Cub Ron Santo. Harry's catch phrase was "Holy Cow!"

Pp is for Parade

P is for Parade, 5 million in the **street,** to celebrate the team that proved they couldn't be **beat.**

The Cubs victory parade attracted over 5,000,000 people, the largest single gathering in US history and the 7th largest in human history.

Q q is for Queasy

Q is for Queasy, which is how we all **felt,**
when the Indians' Rajai Davis had his tying **belt.**

When Rajai Davis hit a two-run homer to tie the game in the 8th inning, fans and players alike were sick to their stomachs, thinking, *Here we go again.*

Rr is for Rossi

R is for Rossi, the man we all call **Gramps.**
His homerun and leadership turned the Cubbies into **champs.**

David Ross, in his final season before retirement, was a father figure to the young team. He also showed he had one more big swing left when he homered to center in Game 7.

Ss

is for the Smile

S is for the Smile that curled Bryant's **lip** as he made the final throw, despite a little **slip.**

As Kris Bryant fielded a little dribbler with two outs in the 10th inning, he had a big smile on his face as he prepared to throw to first to seal victory. The throw was perfect, even though his foot slipped out from under him on the wet grass.

Tt is for Tears

T is for Tears on every girl and **boy.**
The usual tears of sadness were replaced with tears of **joy.**

After over 100 years of heartbreak, the Cubs finally gave fans the ultimate reason to celebrate in 2016.

U u is for the Underwear

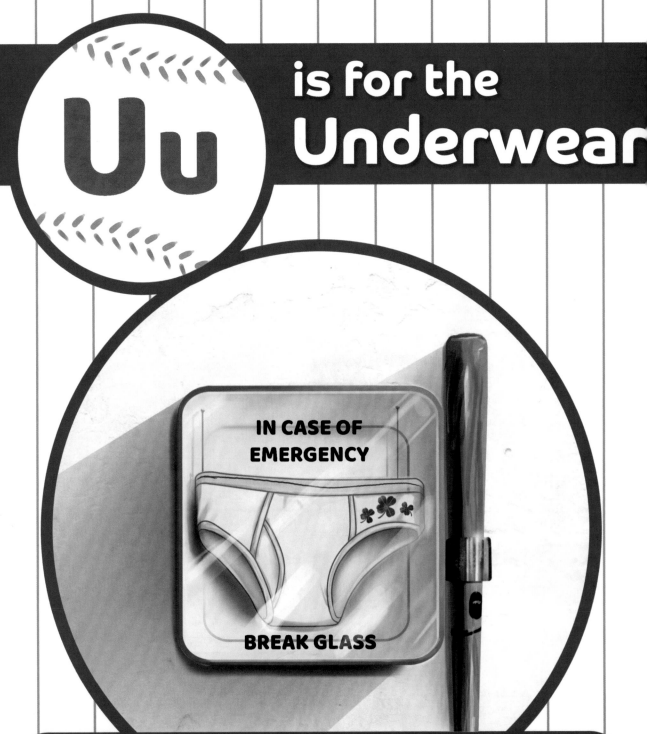

IN CASE OF EMERGENCY

BREAK GLASS

U is for the Underwear that Matt Szczur borrowed **out,** which gave Dexter Fowler a little extra **clout.**

Anthony Rizzo was struggling badly in the postseason until he borrowed bench player Matt Szczur's bat and immediately hit a homerun and caught fire. Dexter Fowler, mired in a slump of his own, borrowed Szczur's underwear to get him going...and it worked!

Vv

is for
Victory

V is for Victory,
finally **complete.**
With a team so young and dandy,
they surely will **repeat.**

After 108 years of waiting, the Cubs finally got the victory everyone was waiting for in 2016.

W w is for Waveland

W is for Waveland, where the ball hawks come to **play.**
They seemed to get a Cub souvenir every single **day.**

Behind the left field wall sits Waveland Avenue. Fans will stand on the street during games, trying to catch Cubs homers that clear the bleachers.

Xx

is for X-Cubs

X is for X-Cubs factor, which is hard to **quantify.**
When the Cubs are actually in it, the theory just runs **dry.**

The X-Cub factor was a theory by sportswriter Jerome Holtzman that said that the team with three or more former Cubs players is destined to lose the World Series. He was usually right.

Yy is for Youth

Y is for Youth, which the Cubs had in **spades,** which should lead in the future to multiple **parades.**

The Cubs were one of the youngest teams in baseball in 2016 and even set a record for the most starting players under 25 in a World Series game.

Zz is for Zobrist

Z is for Zobrist, who did not scare a **bit** when called upon in the 10th to get the biggest **hit.**

Ben Zobrist's hit in the final inning that chased home the lead run was arguably the biggest hit in franchise history.

ABOUT THE AUTHOR

F is for Finally is Robert's debut children's book! He lives in Arlington Heights, Illinois, with his wife Eleni and their two children, Ivy and Wills.